SENECA INDIAN
STORIES

SENECA INDIAN STORIES

By
Ha-yen-doh-nees (Leo Cooper)

Illustrations by Beth Ann Clark

The Greenfield Review Press

SENECA INDIAN STORIES
By Ha-yen-doh-nees (Leo Cooper)

Bowman Books #7
ISBN 0–912678–89–5
Library of Congress # 94–75711

The Greenfield Review Press
Greenfield Center, New York 12833

Distributed by The Talman Company, Inc., 131 Spring St.,
New York NY 10012, 212-431-7175

Contents

How the Crow Got His Black Clothes

"Want to hear how the Crow got his black clothes?" The car was warm and stuffy and after a long ride from eastern Pennsylvania, the children were restless from enforced inactivity.

With that question and implied invitation, however, heads popped up from the back seat, bodies tensed with anticipation, and firm "yes, Yesses" came in reply.

The story-teller was Leo Cooper, Ha-yen-doh-nees (the woodmaker), a Seneca resident of the Allegany Reservation in western New York State. We were on our way from his home in Kill Buck to the Longhouse at Steamburg, New York. He swung around on the passenger side of the front seat so as to face his young audience in back.

"My father told us many stories years ago when we were children growing up on this reservation. His father had told him the stories and his father before him. Nobody wrote them down because the Senecas didn't have reading and writing then. They depended on remembering things, storing them in their heads so they could be told and enjoyed every now and then. That way the stories were passed on from hundreds of

way the stories were passed on from hundreds of years ago.

"Animals didn't always have fur and feathers for clothing. When they were first made, the animals just had skin like you and I do. When winter came the animals got cold and when it rained they got wet so they kept complaining and asking the Creator if something could be done about it.

"One day, Ha-wen-nee-yoh (the Creator) called all the animals together and he said to them 'I have heard your complaining long enough and I have decided to do something about it.' He then opened a big bag he had with him and pulled out a whole batch of beautiful clothes. There were beautiful furs of all colors, feathers that were soft and fluffy and colors of the rainbow, long hair and short hair, and last of all a plain black suit of black feathers. The animals oohed and aahed over all these wonderful things but the crow looked at the black suit and said, 'I pity the one who gets that one!'

"Of course, the animals were eager to try on these beautiful clothes but they couldn't agree who should have what. Ha-wen-nee-yoh wanted them to stop fighting so he told them he would give out the clothes the next morning with the first one awake getting first choice and each one in turn as they woke up.

"All of the animals wanted to be first so they

tried to stay awake as long as they could, hoping to stay awake all night. But it had been an exciting and busy day so they got sleepier and sleepier. One by one they dropped off to sleep. Crow was determined not to fall asleep because he was very greedy and didn't want anybody to be ahead of him. He felt his eyes wanting to close so he put sticks against his eyelids to keep them open. Finally it was too much for him and he fell asleep just before morning.

"When morning came, the animals woke up and one by one made their choice of furs or feathers from the bag of beautiful clothes held by Ha-wen-nee-yoh. But Crow didn't wake up and didn't wake up. He was so tired from having stayed up so late that he was the last one to wake up!

"By the time Crow did wake up, all the beautiful clothes were gone and the only thing left was the plain black suit which nobody wanted. Ha-wen-nee-yoh said very sternly to him: 'you were lazy and woke up last, now you must wear the suit you made fun of for the rest of your life!' That's how the Crow got his black clothes."

By the end of the story our trip was ended and we reached the Longhouse where preparations were being made for that year's strawberry ceremony. As I was parking the car, I said, "Leo, why don't you write those stories down so they won't be forgotten and children everywhere can enjoy them?"

"I just might do that, Dr. Joe" he said as he made his way out of the car.

Today, Leo's journey has ended and he rests under a wild cherry tree near his beloved river. We didn't ever get around to discussing the stories again but before he went on the long trail to the place where good Senecas go to another world he put into writing a number of stories as he remembered them. His reflections on life and growing up on the Allegany Reservation, together with these stories, were found carefully written in an old ledger book. This is the final message of Ha-yen-doh-nees, Heron Clan, Seneca Nation of Indians.

Joseph A. Francello

Foreword

The author in writing this book has endeavored to entertain the reader by relating some of the old tales of Indian folklore and to compare life as it is today on the Allegany Indian Reservation in New York state with the life of the Indian in the early part of the twentieth century.

Seneca heritage is authentically depicted in the chapters on superstitions, dreams, Falseface and medicine societies, witchcraft and the Djogaa-oh or Little People. Great emphasis is placed on these many facets of Indian life and the part they play in the various rituals and festivals celebrated throughout the year.

All the incidents in this book are real and factual experiences of persons either related or personally known to the author.

May this book afford its readers the same pleasure as the author has experienced in creating it.

Howh-nyoh!
Let's get on with it!

Prologue

Ha-yen-doh-nees was a member of the Heron Clan, a member of the Seneca Nation of Indians of N.Y. State, born on the Allegany Reservation and a fourth generation descendant of John O'Bail who was better known as Chief Cornplanter, a war chief of the Senecas in the seventeen hundreds.

Ha-yen-doh-nees was now retired and had returned to the reservation to spend his remaining years of retirement there. One day as summer was changing to fall, he drove his automobile down a private road that ended at the bank of the Allegheny River.

Ha-yen-doh-nees parked his car in the field and walked to the bank of the river and sat looking at the woods, the river and the sky as he had done many times before in his youth and early childhood. The only sounds were the wind in the leaves, the songs of birds, an occasional train, the noise of cars and trucks back on the distant highway, and the sound of occasional planes as they flew overhead on their way to Bradford Airport and other distant cities.

As Ha-yen-doh-nees reclined in the shade of a big oak tree on the river bank he noticed one thing that was missing from the scene and that was the spur line of the Pennsylvania Railroad which in years past followed the opposite bank of the river at the very foot of the hills and connected Olean, New York, and Oil City, Pa., and which had now been abandoned with the construction of the Allegheny River Reservoir project.

New York State was even now negotiating with the Council of The Seneca Nation of Indians to acquire this abandoned railroad right-of-way for an expressway highway.

As Ha-yen-doh-nees rested there in the shade he thought of the many changes that had taken place since the days of his childhood and how different things and conditions were now from what they were then.

He thought of how the children of this day and age had never heard the shrill toot of the steam whistle or the sharp exhaust of a steam locomotive especially on a cold frosty winter night when the trains sounded like they were coming through your backyard. Or how the children of today didn't have to walk two miles to attend a one-room school heated in cold weather by a wood-burning stove, and to drink water hauled from a nearby spring instead of a fountain. He remembered cold winter mornings when, if no sleighs had traveled the road, you broke your own trail through the deep snow to the school-house which was nearly two miles from where you lived. Now, buses picked the school children up at their very doors and transported them to modern central schools which were equipped with cafeterias to feed the students at lunchtime and buses transported them home again after school.

As he thought about all these modern improvements he remembered how it was when he went to school.

In his childhood, Ha-yen-doh-nees lived in a wooden frame building which was two stories high and was made with double walled hemlock boards, the walls and ceiling of which were papered with newspaper neatly pasted on the walls and ceilings in the upstairs part of the house while the downstairs part of the house was papered with wallpaper of various designs. The house lacked indoor plumbing and water was obtained from a hand-operated pump in the yard and carried into the house to be used there.

Cooking and heating was done by means of wood-burning cooking and heating stoves, and it was the work of the smaller children to pump the water and carry in the wood. They also had to feed the chickens and pigs, and whatever other livestock the family owned.

In the fall, his father dug the potatoes, picked

the apples, and dug a big round storage pit in a part of the garden, and placed the potatoes, apples, and cabbage separately in the pit, covered it with a thick layer of hay and covered the entire pit with approximately two feet of earth. When potatoes, or cabbages, or apples were wanted in the winter, part of the earth covering was removed and the vegetables taken out.

He remembered the flavor of apples which were taken from the storage pit; they had a distinctly different flavor and aroma from apples which were not buried. He thought of the wild berry picking in the summer, first wild strawberries, then the wild blueberries, or huckleberries as they were called, and then the wild blackberries all of which were canned for winter use. He remembered the wild foods which he had helped to gather as a child. First, in spring, wild onion for that delicious wild onion soup, leeks which were cooked with pork, cowslips (marsh marigold), and milkweed greens in early summer.

He thought of how the various "doings" at the Longhouse had changed. When he was a child, you attended the "doings" at the Longhouse, and you sat and listened to the preaching and you were made to keep quiet until everything was over; today the children are permitted to run in and out during the preaching and even the adults now sometimes talk so loud that it is difficult for the speaker to be heard, this was just not done in years past.

As he lay there in the shade, Ha-yen-doh-nees remembered the old Indian gentleman who told stories to children and adults. He was an old man—some said he was over a hundred years old when he died. He would come with his pack of Indian medicines, and they were wrapped in a red bandana handkerchief and he also wore a red bandana handkerchief folded into a band about 2 inches wide around his forehead in the manner of the Navajo.

He would come to a house and stay for a week or two usually in the cold weather months. In the summer he camped out in the woods and gathered his herbs, bark, and roots for medicine.

Whenever he came he was given a place to sleep and food, and cast off clothing from the men (shoes, trousers, shirts, coats, and underclothing) and he would carry in the wood and water, and help around by washing and drying dishes, and would even cook when asked to do so.

His coming was eagerly looked forward to both by children and adults. The adults because he had all the latest interesting gossip and news; and the children because of the stories he told.

Gather around young people while Ha-yen-doh-nees repeats the stories which he told.

Many of these stories were about animals. I suppose because the Indians lived very close to nature in the olden days and the animals' habits and lives were familiar to the Nun-da-wah-gah, or people of the hill, by which name the Senecas were known.

How the Rabbit came to have Long Ears and Long Hind Legs

The first story I shall relate is one about Gwah-yonk, the rabbit, and how he came to have long ears and long hind legs. Gwah-yonk was an inquisitive rabbit who would see other animals or people talking together and he would sneak through the brush and weeds to where he could hear every word that was said.

Sometimes the things he heard were nice things and sometimes he heard bad things, but good or bad, Gwah-yonk just couldn't keep from telling all that he heard and many times trouble resulted from his repeating the things he over-heard.

This greatly displeased the Great Spirit, or Ha-wen-nee-yoh (God) and he scolded Gwah-yonk, telling him that he should respect others rights to privacy and that it was wrong to repeat what others might expect to be confidential.

Gwah-yonk, however, would not mend his ways and continued to do as he had always done — wherever two animals or people were talking, he would be nearby listening and later he would repeat what he had heard to anyone who would listen.

One day Ha-wen-nee-yoh decided that because Gwah-yonk would not obey him he should be punished.

Ha-wen-nee-yoh then called the East Wind and the West Wind and together they caught Gwah-yonk's ears and hind legs, and each pulled in opposite directions and stretched Gwah-yonk's ears and hind legs until he cried out in great pain. When the East Wind and the West Wind released Gwah-yonk, his ears were now very long and his hind legs and hind feet were also very long.

Ha-wen-nee-yoh then said to Gwah-yonk, "Now, whenever you try to hide, everyone will see your long ears and when you try to run away your long hind legs and feet will betray you and everyone will know who it is, and say there goes Gwah-yonk."

And that is why all rabbits have long ears and long hind legs and long feet, and run by taking long leaps over the ground.

Why the Rabbit has a Short Tail and Split Lip

This is another story about Gwah-yonk and how he came to have a short tail and a split upper lip.

One day in Autumn, Gwah-yonk was in the forest and it was a beautiful day. As he walked among the trees, Gwah-yonk suddenly felt a great desire to run and sing, and his thoughts turned to winter. Because it was a warm day, he thought how nice it would be if it would only snow a bit today. As he ran, he sang "Ah-nee-yoh! Ah-nee-yoh!"—the Seneca word for snow—"Snow, Snow, how I wish I had snow, how I would run if I had snow!"

After awhile it began to snow and as it snowed, Gwah-yonk ran faster and sang louder "Snow, Snow, how I would run if I had snow," and the faster he ran and the louder he sang, the harder it snowed. Finally he became exhausted and as it was becoming dark night, he crawled into a clump of bushes and fell sound asleep.

What Gwah-yonk didn't know was that as he ran and sang it had snowed harder and harder so that the snow was as deep as the tops of the trees and what Gwah-yonk thought was a clump of bushes was in reality the top of a very big tree.

During the night as Gwah-yonk slept it thawed because it really wasn't winter yet and the snow melted very rapidly. When he awoke in the morning, he found himself stranded high and dry in the top of a big tree.

Gwah-yonk was very hungry and he wished that he was safely on the ground again but he didn't have claws for climbing on his feet so there he was stranded high in the tree. Gwah-yonk finally decided he would have to jump so he closed his eyes and jumped. Now, when he jumped his tail caught on a small branch and broke off very close to his body and he fell head first to the ground where he landed on a rock which split his upper lip.

Gwah-yonk managed to survive his fall but that is why rabbits have short tails, and split upper lips.

Some versions of this tale relate that the tree in which Gwah-yonk spent the night was a willow tree, and that every year before the leaves come back to the trees you can see the white fur of Gwah-yonk's tail among the branches. These are what we call pussy willows but which are really part of a rabbit's tail.

Da-nah-hoh!
It is Finished

Why the Raccoon washes his Food and wears a Mask

Djo-aah-gah was a raccoon who lived in the forest. He was a very mischievous individual and took great pleasure in playing tricks on his neighbors, especially those who were old and not able to retaliate.

Now, there lived in a clearing in the forest an old Indian man and his aged wife. This old Indian always had the best garden because he and his wife worked very hard to keep it free of weeds. His corn, beans and squash were the largest and finest to be found among all the tribe.

One day, as Djo-aah-gah was walking through the forest, he came upon the clearing where the old Indian and his wife were working in their garden. He heard the old man say to his wife, "The corn is now ready for eating and it is the largest and best we have ever grown." His wife replied, "That is true, let us give thanks to the Great Spirit for making our garden the finest in the forest."

Djo-aah-gah listened, he began to think of how he could steal the corn, and at the same time play a trick on the old man and his wife. That night, while everyone was asleep, he crept into the cornpatch and ate all the corn his little stomach would hold. Then he began pulling down the cornstalks which were standing and stripped them of the ears of corn.

When morning came, the old Indian saw what had happened to his cornpatch. He was very angry and vowed to his wife that he would punish whoever was responsible for the damage. He pulled some wild mustard plants from the ground and mashed them into a watery paste. He smeared this paste over the corn that grew on the outer edges of the patch.

That night, Djo-aah-gah returned to the cornpatch and pulled down a stalk and began to eat the first ear of corn. The wild mustard burned his mouth and some went into his eyes. He rolled

in pain in the dirt of the garden and clutched a fistful of cool soil which he put in his mouth to ease the pain. It did ease the pain in his mouth but his eyes still smarted from the mustard. He rubbed his eyes with his paws and smeared the dirt across his face above his nose.

Now, Ha-wen-nee-yoh, the Great Spirit saw what had happened to Djo-aah-gah and he said. "You have been justly punished for the mischief you have done and from this day forth, you will wear a black mask across your face above your nose. Everyone will know why, and you will never again eat without first washing your food to determine that it has not first been smeared with mustard."

That is why all raccoons always wash their food and why they wear a black mask above their noses.

The Woman and the Bear

Once there lived in the forest a huge black bear who took great pleasure in frightening other animals and people because of his great strength and size.

Now, although he had tremendous strength and a huge body, his brain was very small so he wasn't very bright mentally.

There was a little old lady who lived alone in a cabin in the woods, and she was very tiny and weak but mentally alert.

This huge bear one day decided that he would

frighten this little old lady and drive her from her cabin while he laughed in amusement at her fright.

One night he ambled up to the cabin and rapped on the door five times. The woman, thinking that perhaps someone had come to visit her, called out "Dadzoh" which means "come in." Nobody came in and the raps were not repeated. For three nights the same thing happened and the little old woman began to wonder if she were being visited by Djis-gaah (ghosts).

She had never been bothered like this before and being a brave woman, she decided to find out what was rapping on her door. On the fourth day she cut a tiny peephole in the cabin door through which she could see who did the rapping.

That night at the usual time there were the five raps on the door, but this time the woman didn't say "Dadzoh." Instead she quietly went to the door and through the peephole she saw the huge bear. When she did not say "come in" the bear was very surprised. He growled and said, "Is anyone home?"

The little old woman answered, "no, nobody lives here." The bear was disappointed and went away and never returned to the cabin.

Now this proves that a small weak body with an alert brain can always outwit a huge powerful body with a small brain.

Why the Robin's Breast is Red

A party of warriors went on a hunting trip to the North country to kill some moose, both for the meat and for the skins which made strong leather for moccasins and clothing.

When these hunters arrived in the North country it was in the season of the frosty nights and the changing of the leaves to their autumn shades of red and gold.

Upon reaching the moose country, they built a lean-to shelter of logs to protect them from the frosty nights and rainy days. When they had built their shelter they were visited by a robin who stayed near their camp and sang every day.

There were no moose to be found, however, because they had moved farther north to forage for food. The hunting party decided to wait until the moose would return, but days passed into weeks and still there was no sign of the returning moose.

Food supplies began to run low and the hunters, suffering from lack of proper food, became ill and one by one they lay upon the floor of the camp and died. Finally, there was only one hunter left and he too became ill.

He lay helpless on the floor of the shelter beside the fire and waited for death to come. He was too weak to get wood for the fire and finally the fire died out, leaving the hunter sick, cold, and all alone.

The robin, noticing that there was no sign of life in the camp, flew down to see what was wrong and he found the hunter lying very ill beside the remains of the camp fire. The robin flew to the fire and stirred up the ashes and found a spark of fire remaining. He flew away and brought back dry grass and twigs which he placed on the pile of ashes. He then began to fan the ashes with his wings. Just when he was about to give up, he noticed a coal had begun to glow red, so he continued to fan the coal with his wings until the hot coal started burning the grass and twigs.

The robin fanned the little fire with his wings until it grew bigger and he then went and brought larger sticks which he placed upon the fire and fanned some more until he had a good fire burning again.

Only then did he notice that his breast which was once covered with white feathers was now turned to a deep shade of red.

When the fire began to burn again, it heated the camp and the remaining warrior began to feel better, and as he looked there was a fine big moose standing near the camp clearing. He killed the moose with his bow and arrow and after he had roasted and eaten some of the meat, his strength returned rapidly.

As he grew stronger the hunter gathered enough wood to keep the fire going and as the nights became colder the robin roosted on a pole inside the shelter and the hunter shared his food with the robin by hanging strips of suet for him to eat.

The hunter had fine hunting luck and by the time the first snow came, he had enough dried skins and dried meat, so he built a crude sled of branches and boughs on which to haul the meat and skins back to his home lodge.

As he started his trip home, the robin flew

along with him for several days. Then, one day the robin said, "I must leave you now and fly to the warm Southland for the winter, but I will come again when the buds are becoming leaves in the Spring." The hunter thanked him for helping him when he needed help badly and said, "You will always be welcome at my home, so now have a safe trip to warmer country."

Sure enough, when Spring returned a pair of robins built a nest near the hunter's lodge and one of them had a reddish brown breast.

Soon there were four bright blue eggs in the robin's nest and later there were four little robins with red breasts who remained near the hunter's lodge all summer.

Each year the robins returned and nested beside the lodges of their friends and that is how the robin got his red breast!

How the Mice
kept the Peace
among the Tribes

Mice have always lived near the habitation of man; and this was also true in the time before the coming of the White Settlers to the lands of the Indians—when men, animals and trees could speak to each other. The mice had their chiefs, and council to govern themselves and they lived in tribes among the Iroquois.

One day the mice saw that a certain tribe of the Iroquois was gathered in a clearing in the forest, to hold a council session, and they, being curious as to the reason for the council, crept

quietly up to where the Indians were gathered around the council fire, to listen to what the Indians were talking about. It was the season of the year just before the time of the Green Corn harvest dance. One of the Chiefs of the tribe was speaking and the mice heard him say that they must make war upon a neighboring tribe. This War Chief told his listeners that they must prepare to leave that very day. Some of the older chiefs spoke against going to war, and even the clan mothers tried to reason with the War Chief. They said, "You must not go to war against our neighbors for some of you will not return, and there will be great sadness among our people, and the hunting season and the time of harvest are near at hand, and if you do not go out on hunting parties, there will be great hunger and suffering among us when winter comes."

This young War Chief had great influence among the younger warriors, who greatly outnumbered the older chiefs and older warriors and they called for a vote on whether or not to go to war.

A vote was taken in which the young warriors all voted to go to war and so it was decided to leave that very night as soon as the moon had risen.

They all put on their war paint and brought their bows and arrows to the clearing in the forest and placed them on the ground. Then they decided to sleep until the moon had risen and then start out. Now the warriors were fast asleep.

The Chief of the mice called his followers together and they held a Council of mice. The Mouse Chief was a wise old mouse and he knew that if there was to be suffering among the real people, the mice would also suffer, so he made a plan to stop the Indians from going on the warpath.

He said to the other mice, "We can stop this war before it starts if we wait for darkness to fall and before the moon rises, we will destroy their bows and arrows." The other mice agreed to do this, and as soon as it was dark, and while the warriors were asleep, the mice crept up the stockpile of bows and arrows and chewed the rawhide bowstrings and the feather tips of the arrows, making them useless.

The mice then hid themselves nearby to see what would happen. When the moon had risen, the warriors arose and went to where they had left their bows and arrows, only to find them useless.

At first they were very angry, but some of them said, "Ha-wen-nee-yoh, the Great Spirit, did not want us to fight against our neighbors, and he has sent his messengers to punish us for deciding to go upon the warpath."

In the end, the Indians stayed home to harvest the crops and go on hunting parties and Ha-wen-nee-yoh blessed them with a plentiful supply of meat.

That winter the Indians and the mice had plenty to eat and were warm and happy as they waited for the New Year celebration to begin.

How Bats came into Being

Many moons had passed since the mice had stopped a certain tribe of the Iroquois from going upon the warpath against their neighbors. For a time everything was quiet and peaceful and everyone was happy, both among the Indians and the mice, until one day a mouse who was among those who destroyed the Indians' weapons, met with several of his friends and they talked about how strong they were, and that the real people, Ong-weh-onh-weh, were really much weaker than mice.

Now, life had been pleasant and easy for the

mice and just like real people, when life is easy with plenty of food and warmth, many people are easily led into doing mischief, and getting themselves into trouble. So it was with these few mice as they talked and boasted.

One of the mice said to his fellows, "Let us show the Ongweh-onh-weh that we are much more stronger than they, and that we are really their masters.

"By hiding their seed corn which they expect to plant in the Spring, we can cause them to worry, and after awhile we can offer to find their lost seed if they will admit that we are stronger and wiser than they."

The other few mice decided that he was right and so that night when it was dark, they began to carry away the Indians' seed corn and hid it in a dry cave which no Indian had ever seen, and none knew about.

It was hard work, but the mice worked all night and finally the last of the seed corn had been hidden safely in the cave.

Now the mice said, "We will now go to our homes and sleep, and nobody will know who did this." But they were wrong for the West Wind had seen them and knew who they were and he traveled to the Sky-land home of Ha-wen-nee-yoh, the Great Spirit, and told him all that he had seen and who the mice were who stole and hid the Ongweh-onh-weh's (real people) seed corn. This greatly displeased Ha-wen-nee-yoh, who said "I must punish these mice lest they do some greater wrong."

Ha-wen-nee-yoh then called the guilty mice together and told them that he knew what they had done, and that they must be punished. He said to them, "You can no longer be trusted to live among the real people or among mice. Therefore, I will change you into a different animal and you will no longer be mice." The mice hung their head in shame. Ha-wen-nee-yoh continued. "You will no longer have legs to walk with, instead you will have leathery wings to fly about with, and your feet will be attached to your body instead of legs. Because you committed your mischief in the night, you will from now on live and fly about in the night; because you hid the seed corn in a dark cave, you will now live in dark caves, and as you now hang your heads in shame, you will forever sleep by hanging by your feet, upside down from the walls of your cave—you will be called bats."

And now, young people, that is how the bats came into being, why they have no legs, why they have leathery wings and hang upside-down in the dark caves and only fly about at night.

Da-nah-hoh!
It is Finished

Greedy Fawn
and the
Magic Chestnut

A long time ago there grew in the great forest a chestnut tree on which grew magic chestnuts.

These magic chestnuts were in great demand among the Indians because a very small grating from the nut swelled and filled the kettle in which it was being cooked, so that a very small portion of a single magic nut was able to feed an entire large family.

This was considered a blessing from Ha-wen-nee-yoh, the Great Spirit, and the Indians always remembered to thank him for it.

Now there lived in an Indian village a young husband and wife who had a small son named Greedy Fawn who came by his name because his appetite for food never seemed to be satisfied.

One day Greedy Fawn's parents went to work in their garden and they left Greedy Fawn along at home. Before they left, Greedy Fawn's parents cautioned him not to build a fire lest he be injured and they also warned him not to touch the magic chestnut.

Hardly had his parents disappeared down the trail then Greedy Fawn had a fire going and a kettle of water over it. When the water began to boil Greedy Fawn took the magic chestnut and grated a generous portion into the kettle. Immediately, the grated chestnut began to swell and Greedy Fawn said, "Now at last I will have all I want to eat."

Soon the kettle began to boil over and Greedy Fawn stirred the chestnut porridge as he had seen his mother do, but the porridge continued to swell until the kettle was not large enough to contain the porridge.

Greedy Fawn rapped the sides of the kettle with a paddle as his mother did, but now both the kettle and the paddle began to grow bigger and bigger. Greedy Fawn stirred faster and faster but the porridge, the kettle, and the paddle continued to grow bigger. The kettle became so large that Greedy Fawn could not stir the porridge unless he ran around and around the big kettle.

The paddle became heavier and heavier, yet Greedy Fawn dared not stop, and soon his arms grew very tired from stirring the huge kettle with the huge paddle, and his legs ached from running around the kettle.

At last Greedy Fawn fell exhausted beside the kettle and the porridge spilled over the sides and began to fill the wigwam.

Greedy Fawn was now too tired to rise and run away so he began to yell long and loudly for help. Finally, just as he was about to be buried in the porridge, his parents who had heard his loud cries for help, burst into the cabin and rescued him.

They did not have to punish Greedy Fawn for what he had done because he was so frightened because of the close call he had from drowning in the porridge that he never again built a fire or touched the magic chestnut while his parents were away from the wigwam.

Ha-yen-doh-nees, as he thought of the story of Greedy Fawn and the magic chestnut, remembered a time in early manhood when he went to visit his aged father.

As they sat talking on his father's veranda, his father laughed and said, "Something happened to me a few days ago that reminded me of the story of Greedy Fawn and the magic chestnut." Ha-yen-doh-nees said, "Tell me about it."

His father, who lived alone, said, "Well, the other day I bought some beef to make soup for my dinner and the storekeeper asked me what I would put into it. When I told him, he asked if I had ever put barley into the soup and when I said 'No' he showed me some and I bought some to try it.

"I had never used barley before and I put a generous portion into the kettle after I had removed the meat, and just like the magic chestnut, the barley began to swell and to fill the kettle. I began to stir the soup but the barley continued to swell until it too ran over the sides of the kettle and I began to think of Greedy Fawn and the magic chestnut.

"When the barley stopped swelling, I had no soup in the kettle, only a kettle full of barley much of which I fed to the dog."

Ha-yen-doh-nees thought that the story of Greedy Fawn must be a very old story because his father was about 80 years old then and he had heard the story in his childhood.

Why Owls
are so much
like Cats

The common house cat, Dah-go-geeh, has always been a friend to man and the Ongweh-onh-
weh (the real people, the Senecas) believe that
the Ha-wen-nee-yoh (The Great Spirit) sent him
to live among the real people to help them keep
the mice and chipmunks and other rodents from
overrunning the earth because they multiply so
fast and if the cats were not on hand to reduce
the rodent population, the real people would not
be able to raise enough corn, beans, and other
grain to feed everyone.

Now there was a pair of Dah-go-geeh who lived among the Indians and who loved the real people and kept the mice, chipmunks, and other rodents from stealing too much corn or destroying other vegetables which the real people had stored for winter use.

They lived happily with an old Indian and his wife who fed them from their own table and they slept beside the fire and played about the cabin. In fact they were a part of the family and the old Indian and his wife loved them and petted them and kept them well-fed. Through many years these cats lived with the old couple and finally became old and died of old age. This grieved the old couple who sadly mourned their loss and the were unhappy because the cats were gone.

Now, Ha-wen-nee-yoh (the Great Spirit) saw how lonely the old couple were especially at night when they yearned for the presence of the cats, and because the cats were faithful friends to the old couple, Ha-wen-nee-yoh decided that he would let them return to the earth but in a different form.

Accordingly, he put the spirits of the two cats into two birds which he called Gwa-oh (owls) and they returned to earth in their new bodies but they had eyes like cats and could see in the dark like cats, and they ate mice and other small rodents.

One evening, as it was becoming dark, the old couple sat outside their cabin and noticed two birds which flew to the roof of the cabin and then to the yard where the old couple sat. They began to play and tumble about as they did when they were cats, and the old couple watching them saw how much they resembled their Da-go-geeh who had left them. They hurried into the cabin and brought out some food in the dish which they used to feed the cats.

The Gwa-oh ate and then they told the old couple that Ha-wen-nee-yoh had sent them to be with the old couple and that they would always be near them to help keep the mice and other rodents from overrunning the Indian village.

The old couple were again happy and were always kind to the Gwa-oh because they knew that their beloved Da-go-geeh had returned to them. And that, young people, is how the Gwa-oh (owls) came into being and why they can see in the dark like cats, and why they help to keep the mice and other rodents from eating up the real people's corn and other stored vegetables.

Why Dah-Go-Geeh (Cats) eat first and then wash

One day Day-go-geeh, the cat, caught a mouse and made ready to eat it, but just as he was about to take his first bite, the mouse said, "Wait!" "Why should I wait? said Dah-go-geeh, "I've waited long enough and I'm very hungry."

The mouse answered, "No brave warrior ever eats until after he has first washed his hands and face." Dah-go-geeh then put the mouse down and began to wash his face. The mouse jumped up and scampered away and Dah-go-geeh lost his dinner, and being angry at losing his dinner,

40

Dah-go-geeh said, "This has taught me a lesson, I will never wash until after I have eaten" and that is why cats always eat first and then wash after they have eaten.

Why Crows steal Corn and have no Home

A long time ago, when the Ha-wen-nee-yoh (The Great Spirit) decided to give the Ongweh-onh-weh (the real people) food that they could eat fresh and which could also be stored to sustain them during the long winter months, he created the corn.

He then called upon the birds to send someone to his Skyland home to carry the corn back to the real people on earth.

Now, Gah-gah, the crow, always has maintained that a crow was chosen to make the long

journey to the Skyland home of the Great Spirit and that he carried the first kernel of corn in his ear to give to the real people to plant.

The crows were a shiftless lot and never provided food for themselves to eat during the cold winter and they flew to the warm southland when food became scarce and even so, many were too lazy and shiftless to make the trip.

A common practice among the real people at planting time is to place three kernels of corn in each hill, and they said, "one for the worm, one for the crow, and one for me."

No matter how many council sessions the crows hold and no matter how many resolutions they make to plant a crop of corn for themselves the next year, and build permanent homes to live in, they never do, and each winter finds them poor and hungry and homeless, waiting again for next Spring planting season to come. Ha-yen-doh-nees remembered an old Indian man who worked very hard and then spent his money having a fine time in the taverns drinking with his friends. Because he would not provide food or a home for himself, he always stayed with relatives whom he visited by turns, accepting food and old clothing from them.

Ha-yen-doh-nees remembers meeting the old man in the city one day and asking him how he was and what he was doing. The old man replied,

"I now live like an old crow. I have no home, and like the crow who flies from tree to tree, I go from one relative to the next for food and lodging."

One day the old man died and was buried in the Indian community cemetery beside a tree there, and Ha-yen-doh-nees visits the cemetery often and has noticed that nearly every time he has visited the cemetery there is usually a flock of crows in the tree beside the old man's grave and he remembers what the old man once told him.

About Djo-Gaa-Oh
(The Little People)

The Indians have their version of Fairies, Elves, or Leprechauns whom they call Djo-gaa-oh (The Little People). The Djo-gaa-oh are supposed to be very powerful and possess supernatural powers. It is said that they are able to reward for doing good, punish for doing evil, right wrongs, and are especially concerned about the affairs of children. They also help the plants to grow, the fruit to ripen, and to assist the Ong-weh-onh-weh (The Real People) in finding and making medicines from the right barks, roots, leaves and plants. They were highly regarded by the real people and many stories are told of happenings and events that involved Djo-gaa-oh.

Ha-yen-doh-nees remembers that when one of his older sisters was a child, his family became involved with Djo-gaa-oh and it happened in this manner.

His family lived in a house at the end of a long lane about 200 yards from the main highway, and one day his sister who was about five or six years old was sitting in the doorway of the little frame house, and as she sat there she saw two children, a boy and a girl, walking along the road that led from the gate to the river.

They were coming from the direction of the river and as she watched they approached the gate and turned down the lane that led to the house. As they came nearer the house, his sister hid her bare feet under her skirt and called their mother and said, "There are two children, a boy and a girl coming." Her mother looked and said, "I don't see them." His sister then said, "There they are, by the apple tree." "Mom, they want me to come play with them." Her mother said, "Did you hear them ask you to come and play with them?" His sister said, "Yes, I did." Her mother said, "You had better come into the house," and as she said this the little boy and girl turned around and started to walk back in the direction

from which they had come. Ha-yen-doh-nees said that his mother was alarmed about what his sister had seen, and told the neighbors what had happened and one of the old women said that what his sister had seen were Djo-gaa-oh and that they would have to have a ceremony for her which they did. Nothing happened to his sister and she never saw the little boy and girl again, but that she never forgot about the little boy and girl and what happened.

He then thought about another incident which happened to one of his neighbors. This man was walking along the railroad tracks one night in early winter when he was waylaid by two men whom he recognized. They struck him on the head with a club and dragged his body to a swamp that bordered the railroad tracks and left him unconscious there.

When the man regained consciousness, there were "little people" pulling him by the hands and saying "Sut geh" which in Seneca means "Get up." When the man tried to arise from the ground, he found that he was unable to do so because his clothing was frozen to the ground.

The little people noticed this and worked and pulled his coat and trousers until they were able to free him. In the meantime he had lapsed into a light sleep and the little people again pulled his hands and arms and told him again "Sut geh" and this time he was able to regain his feet but he didn't know which way to go as he was in the swamp and it was a very dark night and he couldn't see well in the darkness. The little people said, "Neh-ko-gwak" "This way" and led him out of the swamp and to the railroad tracks.

Once back at the railroad tracks he knew where he was and he staggered wounded and very cold to his home where he related to his family what had happened to him and said that if it hadn't been for the Djo-gaa-oh, he would have frozen to death in the swamp.

He believed in Djo-gaa-oh and was grateful to them ever after during the remainder of his life.

Note: Even today, on a nearby reservation, ceremonies pertaining to Djo-gaa-oh are conducted in conjunction with the Dark Dance which is a highly secret function of the medicine society.

Mourning Doves

Once, there was a strong, handsome, young warrior who was loved by everyone in the village where he lived.

This young warrior was a very successful hunter and always shared the game he killed with his neighbors, especially the older couples and the people who were too old to hunt any more. He always caught the most and biggest fish with his spear, and in his fish traps, and these he would also share with others. He would often stop to cut firewood or to draw fresh water from a spring for the old people and for the widows.

Everyone was happy when this handsome, kind, young warrior took a beautiful young Indian girl from the opposite clans to be his wife. This young couple were ideally suited to each other and they built themselves a fine small house. They were very happy together for they truly loved each other.

They had been married only a short time when the young warrior took to the warpath to war against another tribe a great distance from their village.

When the warriors returned from the warpath, they brought news that the young warrior whom everyone loved and respected had been killed in battle. His young and pretty widow was very sad and lonely without him, and one day she slipped quietly away into the forest where she killed herself by eating wild parsnips which are deadly poisonous.

The entire village mourned the loss of the fine young couple who had passed on so early in life, and life in the village was saddened.

Then one day the people noticed a pair of birds sitting on the roof of the house where the young couple had lived. These strange birds did not sing but uttered mournful sounds as they sat on the roof. The birds remained near the house of the young couple and finally the people of the village decided that the Creator had reincarnated the handsome warrior and his wife in the form of birds.

The birds soon became the main topic of conversation in the village and the people fed them from their tables, remembering how the young warrior had always shared his game with everyone.

The birds thrived and built a nest in the eaves of the house where the young warrior and his wife had lived. They soon reared a brood of young birds which are now known as mourning doves by their mournful cries.

How the Real People learned about Medicines

A long time ago, the Ongweh-onh-weh (Real People) did not know how to heal sickness, and because they did not know how to heal themselves, many died when they became ill.

Ha-wen-nee-yoh (The Great Spirit) saw this and feeling sorry for his creation, he sent one of his messengers from the Great Skyland to help them. This is how it happened. One day, an old man approached an Indian village beside the river. He stopped at the first bark house in the village and told the people who lived there that he was very tired and hungry, and that he also was very ill.

He asked if they would take him in and help him. The people answered "No!" They could not be bothered with a sick old man, and that he should try the next bark house and ask them to help him. The old man went from bark house to bark house asking to be taken in and fed and cared for—but it was always the same story. Some said that they were too busy, others said that they were afraid that they, too, might become ill, others said no and told him to move on.

At last, he came to the bark house of an old woman, a member of the Bear clan who lived alone. The old man asked if he might be permitted to come in and lie beside the fire and rest his tired old body. Now, this old woman was kind to everyone, and always helped those who came to her in trouble. She told the old man to come in and rest while she prepared him some warm food to eat. The old man told her that he was very ill and asked her if she would go out into the woods and gather certain roots and bark which would make him well again.

The woman did as he asked and she remembered what he had told her to gather for him. When she returned to her house, the old man told her how to prepare the things which she had brought, which she did. He said, "this is Oh-noh-qua-se (medicine)" and told her what illness it would cure.

The woman asked him to remain with her until he was well enough to travel again, and he agreed. The old man stayed many moons with the woman and during this time became ill many times. Each time, the illness was different, and each time the old man told the woman what to get that would cure the illness and how to prepare it. All these things the woman remembered. Then, one day the old man said to the woman, "You have been very kind to me, and now I must tell you a secret.

"Ha-wen-nee-yoh has sent me to teach Ong-weh-onh-weh (the real people) how to heal sickness and injuries that they might be well and happy. Because you were the only one who would take me in and help me, the people of the Bear clan will be blessed by Ha-wen-nee-yoh, and you of the Bear clan will be the great healer of the people. You will teach others what plants, roots, and bark to gather, how to prepare them, and how much to use, to heal themselves of sickness and injury."

He then said, "Now I must return to Ha-wen-nee-yoh and tell him that I have carried out his orders." He thanked the old woman for her kindness to him, and he told her that she would always be warm and comfortable, and that she would live to a ripe old age. He left the bark house and the woman watched him disappear into the forest as quietly as he had come.

That is how the Ongweh-onh-weh (the real people) learned how to make medicine.

Conclusion

As he reclined there on the bank of the river, Ha-yen-doh-nees suddenly became aware of the fact that he was cold, his hips and legs had begun to ache and he was very hungry. He looked around and saw that the sun no longer shone in the area beside the river and that it had already disappeared behind the hill.

Looking at his wristwatch he noted that it was already past five o'clock. Only then did he realize that he had spent nearly the whole day there beside the river, thinking about and reliving other years now long past.

As he walked painfully back to where he had parked the car, he realized he had forgotten to take his arthritis medication and so had missed two doses.

As he reached the car, he turned to look once more at the river and the hills behind which the sun had set, and suddenly he was happy and glad he had spent the greater part of the day there beside the river.

As he turned the car around, he could see the quarter moon already rising over the hill in the East and he thought of others who had gone before him and had seen that same moon rising in the same place. He thought of other generations, yet unborn, who would see that same moon rising in the same place, but then, he too would be gone from the scene. Those unborn generations would never know that he had passed this way. Things would be entirely different for them.

Ha-yen-doh-nees decided then and there to write this book of stories which you have read. It is hoped you too might share in the pleasure of relating them to others.

Da-nah-hoh!
It is finished

Leo Clifton Cooper was a man of many facets and talents. He possessed a strong will and rugged physique with which he was able to overcome a series of setbacks and misfortunes which began early in his life with the death of his mother when he was only eleven months old.

He was a native American born to Seneca-Iroquois parents (Heron Clan) on the Allegany Reservation in the town of Carrollton, New York. There were eleven children, he being the youngest, and then at the age of three he was taken to the Thomas Indian School on the Cattaraugus Reservation. Shortly after that his oldest sister brought him back home to the family.

A man of great humor, he decided he should have three days of birthdays. A mix-up in the Bureau of Indian Affairs listed his birthday as February 11, 1909 when it should have been the ninth of that month. All attempts to change it proved futile so he decided he should have presents and celebrations on all three days, even in later years.

His formal education began in a one-room schoolhouse at Kill Buck, New York. Later he attended Salamanca High School but quit school when he reached sixteen years of age. After that he worked at a number of jobs, finding time to play baseball, as he was a fierce competitor in that sport.

Much of his work was in structural steel which is ironical since his Indian name, Hi-yen-do-neese, means the woodmaker. He worked as a boiler-maker, bridge-builder, and ship-fitter first class at the shipyards in Buffalo, New York.

A great reader, he studied avidly and acquired an excellent vocabulary, even teaching himself German, Spanish, and Italian. Upon retirement, he moved back to the Allegany Reservation and became involved in politics. He served as counselor, clerk, and then President of the Seneca Nation of Indians.

Active in Masonic affairs, he was Secretary of the Salamanca Masonic Lodge and belonged to the Jamestown Consistory becoming a 32nd degree Mason. Leo served as an elder of the Presbyterian Church on the Reservation while at the same time he held high respect for the traditional Longhouse Religion and the people active in that worship.

The Army Corps of Engineers made him their liaison with the Seneca Indians at the time of the building of the Kinzua Dam in the 1960s.

His marriage to a German-American Woman (Marion) from Buffalo, N.Y. was blessed with one child, Sue, and he became a devoted grandfather to her children Scotty and Stephanie Swetland.

Throughout his life, Leo Cooper practiced the utmost honesty, trust and sincerity. He gave to all the local churches whether he belonged to them or not and at his death he was prayed for in every church in the community. To have known him was an unforgettable experience and a pleasure.

Joseph S. Francello

About the Artist

Beth Ann Clark is a member of the Seneca Nation of Indians, Allegany Reservation, Salamanca, New York. She is of the Deer Clan.

She was born at Springville, New York and spent her youth in Great Valley, New York. She presently calls Salamanca her home.

She obtained her Arts Associates degree from the Olean Campus of Jamestown Community College in 1990. She has been awarded for her art work on the county and state levels and was the illustrator for *One More Story*, a collection of Contemporary Seneca Tales of the Supernatural by Duce Bowen, published by Bowman Books in 1991.